FOR HER
Spy Only

A MASQUERADING MISTRESSES NOVELLA

FOR HER
Spy Only
A MASQUERADING MISTRESSES NOVELLA

ROBYN DEHART

Entangled Publishing, LLC
644 Shrewsbury Commons Ave
STE 181
Shrewsbury, PA 17361
rights@entangledpublishing.com

Amara is an imprint of Entangled Publishing, LLC.

Edited by Kate Fall
Cover design by Heidi Stryker

Manufactured in the United States of America

First Edition July 2014

To my readers who have stuck with me from the beginning, this one is for you. Thank you for your loyalty and your enthusiasm.

And as always to my sweet husband, Paul. You are the love of my life and I wouldn't want to be on this adventure with anyone but you.

Prologue

Miss Winifred Wilmington pulled her green velvet cloak tighter around her. She exhaled and the puff of air was visible, so cold was it inside the carriage.

"We are going to die in here," her maid, Polly, wailed.

Winifred rolled her eyes heavenward. "I seriously doubt that," she said. "It is rather cold, but I suspect someone will be along soon enough and rescue us."

"I could remind you that it was my suggestion that we leave earlier in the day. Or yesterday," Polly grumbled. "It is the eve of Christmas, who else is traveling?"

The thought had crossed Winifred's mind as well, but she certainly wouldn't put voice to it. "Holmes went to search for help. Certainly he will find someone to assist us."

There was no need to panic, as that would solve nothing. Therein lie the significant difference between herself and her longtime maid. Winifred was nothing if not practical. It was a skill she had learned out of necessity. One did not get jilted at the altar without adjusting one's expectations of life and other people. In any case, she was somewhat concerned about being stranded in this frigid carriage all night, though she was hopeful that someone would come along to save them.

Polly sat up. "Do you hear that?"

Polly was so apt at creating drama, no doubt the woman thought she heard wolves outside. "What?" Winifred asked.

"A carriage is coming," Polly said.

Winifred strained her ears, and certainly enough it did sound as if wheels were drawing nearer. Hope bloomed in her chest. The wheels rumbled and the horse hooves clattered louder and louder until they were upon them before they rolled to a stop.

"As long as it's not a highwayman, I suppose we can consider ourselves rescued," Winifred said.

Polly gasped, her hand going to her throat. "A highwayman!"

A male voice sounded outside the carriage, obviously speaking with his party unless Holmes had found this particular someone to salvage them.

There came a rap at the door. Winifred leaned forward and opened it.

A tall gentleman stood there in a great coat with a top hat perched upon his head. He held a cane in his hand. "Madams," he said, the timber in his voice deep and rich.

A chill skirted over Winifred's arms despite the cloak encasing her body. "Good evening, sir," she said. "I hope my driver, Holmes, didn't get you out of bed to rescue us."

"I beg your pardon, I know no such man. I came upon your rig by happenstance."

"Well, then, I should thank you for stopping to assist us. Can our carriage be repaired?"

"I do not know, nor am I inclined to look," he said.

That wasn't very gentlemanly of him. She opened her

mouth to tell him precisely that—

"I will offer you a ride," he said before she could comment.

Winifred considered his words. It wasn't a perfect solution, but it would do. "Yes, my grandmother's estate is not far from here. We would very much appreciate it."

"No," he said.

She started to thank him for his hospitality and then his words sank in. "I beg your pardon? Did you or did you not offer us a ride?"

"To where *I* am going. I am not a coach for hire." He tapped his cane against his chest.

She had the childlike urge to mock him, but thought better of it. Her options for getting out of this predicament were rather limited, so she best mind her manners.

"In the morning, you may have the carriage take you to your destination," he continued. "But in this weather, I am going nowhere else."

"And where is it that you're going?" Winifred asked.

"Coventry Hall," he said.

Nerves prickled at her neck, standing the little hairs on end. "You are?" Winifred asked.

"Alistair Devlin, Marquess of Coventry," he said with only a shadow of a bow.

"Oh good heavens," Polly said, finally breaking her silence. She shook her head violently. "Miss Wilmington, we mustn't go with him. We can wait for Holmes."

"Don't be rude, Polly."

"Yes, don't be rude, Polly," he repeated. "I don't believe you'll have any other options tonight." His shoulders rose in a slight shrug. "Though you could certainly choose to stay here and freeze," he said. "I have made the offer." He turned on his heel and walked away.

"Miss Wilmington, you know what they say of him," Polly said once he was out of earshot. She gripped Winifred's arm tightly. "Mary, who works for Lord Garrick, says she knows the housekeeper that used to work at Coventry. He is a killer," she whispered. "Murdered his own wife, tossed her right off a cliff, they say."

"Don't be so dramatic." But of course Winifred had also heard those rumors and plenty more when it came to the Marquess of Coventry. He had a most interesting reputation. Of course the fact that he rarely, if ever, was seen in London, only fueled said rumors.

Unfortunately the man was right. The odds of someone else coming along to rescue them were very slim. "It is a good offer," Winifred said. "Our only offer, as it were."

"He could be dangerous," Polly warned.

"He is a peer of the realm. Rumor or not, there is a code of etiquette." When Polly looked unconvinced, Winifred continued. "Consider that being tossed off a cliff should result in a rather quick death, whereas freezing in this carriage would be slow and painful, I suspect."

Polly closed her eyes and shook her head as if warding off the image.

"Excuse me, I should like to get down please," Winifred called out. Nerves fluttered in the pit of her stomach, though it could have been the chill from the opened carriage door. Several breaths passed before a footman appeared to assist her to the ground. "Oh, you must be one of the marquess's men. Thank you."

The man nodded, but said nothing. The snow swirled around her, soft as a whisper, covering her face and sticking to her eyelashes. She put her hands in her muff and walked quickly toward the other carriage.

Polly raced up to meet her. "Miss Wilmington, think of your reputation."

"Don't be silly. I am a spinster who was jilted. Besides, my reputation has already been damaged. Furthermore, my reputation certainly won't matter if I freeze to death, now will it?"

"I shall not ride with that man," Polly said with a firm nod of her head.

"Suit yourself, you can wait for Holmes. Do try to stay warm," Winifred said.

"If you go with him, I shall resign," Polly warned.

"Don't bother, I shall simply dismiss you," Winifred said.

Polly made a growling noise, yet still followed behind. "I shall come with you to keep you safe, but I refuse to ride inside with him."

"Do whatever you wish. I am riding inside where it promises to be nice and cozy."

And with that a gloved hand reached out of the carriage door. She took a deep breath, placed her hand in his, and climbed into the carriage. A lantern hung from a hook, illuminating the interior. She took a seat on the plush bench across from the marquess. "Thank you for your hospitality."

"I instructed my footman to stay and wait for your driver."

He certainly did not appear to be murderous. Not that she had any notion of what a murderer might do or say.

"Your maid, she is going to ride outside?" he asked.

"She's a stubborn lot," Winifred said.

"You sacked her," he said.

"Third time this week." She waved her hand dismissively. "Polly and I have plenty of disagreements."

He nodded, then picked up the book that had been sitting on the seat next to him. The carriage lurched forward.

She eyed her unlikely travel companion. He wasn't a friendly sort; formidable was more what she'd consider him. He was tall and lean and imposing, but younger than she had expected. She'd heard of the Marquess of Coventry, but had never before seen him. His reputation in London was notorious. He could not be more than thirty. His cane leaned against the bench next to him, and his gloved hand held onto the gold knob on top. An ugly scar slashed across his left cheek, leading up to his eye.

He looked up from his reading as if he sensed her perusal. His eyes were a startling shade of green, like the first bloom of spring after a blistering winter.

"My name is Winifred Wilmington," she said dumbly.

"Indeed," he said, then went back to his reading.

She felt her brow furrow. "What are you reading?" she asked.

"Shakespeare. *As You Like It*," he said.

She was quiet for a moment, trying to recall if she'd read that particular play. It seemed she must have, but she couldn't recall a single thing about it.

"You know I am not afraid of you," she said. Her mother used to chastise her about her chattiness, but Winifred had a tendency to talk when she was nervous. And the marquess's silence had her quite addled. "I don't think it's very intelligent to believe everything you hear about a person."

"I see," he said, not bothering to look up from his book.

"Oh yes, people are quite spiteful with the rumors they spread." She forced herself to stop talking as she was about to tell him a particularly nasty rumor, but that would be gossiping. She knew she became chatty when she was nervous, and she certainly did not need to say something she would later regret. And she knew the sting of being on the other end of those rumors. When Theodore had left her standing alone with the priest and the church full of onlookers, people had made all sorts of conclusions.

"What is it that people say about me?" he asked, again not looking up from his book.

She studied him for a moment, trying to gauge if he was toying with her. He must know what people said. Even the servants gossiped about him.

He looked up at her and once again she was caught in those unusual eyes. His right brow rose expectedly.

She swallowed. "That you murdered your wife." Her voice came out weak.

"But you do not believe that," he said.

"No, I do not." She shook her head. "You are obviously a responsible and kind gentleman."

"*You* do not know me," he said. He set his book aside. His glove gripped the gold knob on his cane.

"No, but you stopped to assist a stranded lady. That says volumes about your character, my lord," she said, quite pleased with her logic.

He leaned forward, his eyes narrowed. "How do you know I'm not taking you to my castle to ravish you?"

She sucked in her breath. His words should have driven fear into her heart. They should have made her second-guess climbing into this carriage with him. Instead she became acutely aware of how she must look with her traveling cloak and bonnet. She resisted the urge to pat her hair.

"Are you? Going to ravish me, that is?" she couldn't help asking. No man had ever been so forthcoming with her, and the effect was rather intoxicating.

He crooked his finger at her, beckoning her forward.

Curiosity gripped her. She leaned toward him. He had lovely eyes, mossy green with long lashes.

He grabbed her by the chin and pulled her closer, then caught her mouth in a kiss. So shocked by the touch, her lips parted, giving him a brazen invitation to deepen the kiss. His lips were soft and unfamiliar, yet seductive, intoxicating. Her eyes fluttered closed and her hands gripped the fabric of his great coat around his shoulders. And then the kiss was over, ending as quickly and abruptly as it had begun. He leaned back in his seat and she was left in the middle of the carriage with her eyes closed, no doubt looking very much the goose.

"You should not be so trusting," he said.

He was right. Of course he was right. Yet, she felt no fear with him, even at the liberty he had just taken. She felt only curiosity and something that was probably desire, at the very least attraction and intrigue. "You never answered my question," she shot back once she'd regained her senses.

"Which was?"

"If you were intending to ravish me once we arrived at your castle?"

His lips quirked up in a half smile. "I suppose you'll have to wait and see."

Winifred wasn't certain what she'd been expecting of Coventry Hall, but it was quite luxurious for a looming cliffside castle. The room she'd been given hosted a huge four-poster bed, elegantly carved and covered in the richest of fabrics. The fireplace, already lit, heated the room, and a plush carpet covered the stone floor. If she closed her eyes and concentrated hard, she imagined she could hear the waves crashing into the cliffs below.

Despite the rumors, the Marquess of Coventry was most certainly not what she would have expected. She wouldn't deem him charming, but rather appealing. His face wasn't one that most might consider dashing, with his dark features and sharp angles—and that scar. But there was something so alluring in his thickly lashed green eyes. He was mysterious, and she found that attractive.

When they'd arrived at the castle, he'd suggested she get changed, warm up, and then come back down to the dining hall for a light meal. She crept out into the corridor and followed it to the stairs that wound down to the second floor, where he'd said she'd find the dining hall. The castle was quiet, without many servants milling about. Candles sat in sconces against the walls lighting her way.

The rich aroma of food caught her attention and she followed the scent until she reached two large wooden doors. She opened one and peeked inside. A massive table bisected the room, and on one end a sideboard sat covered with dishes of food. Her host already sat at the head of the table, and a footman served him a plate.

The marquess looked up at her. "Are you coming in or not?"

"Yes," she said stupidly. She chose the seat to his right and immediately a footman brought her a plate. "This is your light meal?" She pointed to the heaping platters on the sideboard.

"The cook didn't know what you would eat." He shrugged, bringing attention to his broad shoulders. "We don't receive many visitors here." Though the dining room was rather large, his deep voice curled around her, an echo of the intimacy of their dinner.

The rest of their meal went by with little conversation. The food was delicious, but all Winifred could think about was her impulsive question in the carriage. Asking him if he intended to ravish her. What had she been thinking?

She'd been thinking about that kiss. A spontaneous and passionate, albeit brief kiss between strangers. It had been more enthralling than any of the embraces she'd shared with Theodore. Though he'd been her fiancé for nearly half of a year, he'd never done more than give her chaste kisses that left her cataloging things she had left to accomplish that day. But the marquess's kiss had evoked thoughts and sensations that left her only wanting more.

More of him.

And had her thinking of the ridiculous. Of suggesting that he should ravish her. What would it matter? Her prospects of marriage had already been ruined. Who would care if she gave her body to an attractive stranger in a mysterious castle on the eve of Christmas?

He pushed his chair back from the table and stood.

"What is it you normally do after you eat?" she asked, coming to her feet as well.

He pinned her with those intense eyes of his. "Retire to my study and read."

"Splendid, I very much enjoy a good book."

Was a study a good place to host a seduction? She certainly had no notion, but it was worth an effort. Was she actually intending to do this? She took a deep breath and nodded as if agreeing with herself. The worst he could do was say no.

The room reminded her much of the comfortable study of her father's closest friend, the royal cartographer Sir Reginald Mirren. She took in heavy wooded panels, floor-to-ceiling bookshelves, and a large, imposing desk. But what the marquess had in his study that she had not seen before were the medals. Several of them graced one shelf, and they gleamed in the candlelight.

"Were you in the military?" she asked.

He glanced up from his book and nodded. "I work for the Crown."

"Still? You are active? Are you a captain?"

"I have no classification. I merely work for the Crown."

She wasn't certain what that meant, but he seemed finished with the conversation, so she allowed it to drop.

It took her the better part of thirty minutes once they were settled in the library—him in a large leather chair, her in a softer chaise—to pull together the nerves to approach the subject.

She cleared her throat.

He did not look up from his reading, no longer the

Shakespeare, but now a book from Sophocles.

"I should tell you," she began. "That is, I want you to know that I am open to the possibility of being ravished."

That stole his attention from Sophocles, though aside from one cocked eyebrow, his expression was unreadable. "I beg your pardon?"

"Well, I find myself quite intrigued by the kiss we shared, and if you do not object, I should like to explore—"

"Are you trying to seduce me?" he asked. His tone spoke of surprise, but certainly a man as confident as he would not be caught unaware by a woman taking a fancy to him.

"I am. Though perhaps not successfully. You seem surprised."

"Surprised by your boldness, perhaps."

"I know it is unbecoming for a woman to be so bold," she said, suddenly feeling quite embarrassed and wishing a hole would open in the floor and swallow her.

He set his book aside and stood. "On the contrary." He took a step toward her. "I find your brazenness refreshing."

Warmth spread through her arms and legs.

"What of your reputation?" he asked.

"Well, it would seem that I have recently been accused of being a wanton harlot." She swallowed hard. It had taken her several months to learn to ignore the stares when she shopped for new dresses on Bond Street. And her invitations to social gatherings had all but dried up. "I was thinking that if I have to endure such rumors, I should get to behave thus at least once."

The marquess eyed her a moment, then tipped his head back and laughed riotously. "Miss Wilmington, you are most assuredly a refreshing female. Why is it that people claim you are a wanton?" He held up one finger. "Though I could point out that if this is not your first proposed seduction, that could be the reason."

"No, of course not." She smiled in spite of herself. "This is the first time…that is, you are the first man I have proposed such a thing." She inspected her fingernails, concerned that if she told him the truth about Theodore that he might decline her offer. "I was engaged and my would-be groom left me at the altar. He then told people that he'd done so because he'd discovered me in the arms of another man. A blatant lie, but it would seem that people don't care about my side of the story."

"Is this seduction your way of trapping me into marriage?" He took a couple steps closer to her. "Because as you've heard, I had to kill my first wife to get out of that union."

She laughed.

"Most people don't find me amusing."

She stepped closer to him, so close that she could feel the heat radiating off his body. "I'm not most people."

"Why me? Why seduce me?"

She looked up and was caught in the depths of his green gaze. "I find you intriguing and attractive. And judging by my reaction to the kiss in the carriage, it is safe to say that I desire you."

"I see." He was quiet for a moment, as if weighing her argument. "I have precautions to ensure you will not get with child."

Her heart fluttered. "Does that mean you accept?"

"I am a peculiar sort, Miss Wilmington, a bit of a recluse, most say. I much prefer the company of books to that of people." He laced his fingers with hers. "But I am still a man and when a beautiful woman offers herself to me, I shall gladly accept."

Chapter One

Alistair Devlin, accused murderer, recluse, master code-breaker, and secret spy for the Crown of England, loathed the bustle and noise of the city. Two weeks ago, when fellow members of the Seven, the elite group of spies working to uncover a traitor who'd infiltrated the English government, had brought him Lord Comfry's journal, Alistair had assumed he'd be able to decipher the code quickly.

Despite Alistair's usual ease with codes, this one was proving more challenging, and he had yet to decode the murdered man's journal. The worst part of these two weeks was that he had spent them in London. There were far too many people, not to mention the stench from the streets permeated the air, but the worst part was the ignorance of nearly everyone around him.

Alistair was quite accustomed to being the most intelligent man in the room. It had been this way since he'd been a young man, and he had never had an easy time at accepting the mental limitations of others. He had no patience for idiots.

The good news was, he finally realized why he'd struggled with this particular code.

He'd been approaching the code incorrectly. He had been using every code he'd collected since he began working for the Crown. He'd finally realized that the code was actually rather simple and the random numbers and letters were, in fact, latitude and longitude coordinates. He needed only the help of Sir Reginald Mirren, the royal cartographer.

He tapped his cane on the top of his Hessian boot and waited for the carriage to stop. He had only made the acquaintance of Sir Reginald Mirren on a handful of occasions; the man was the best cartographer in London. He'd been commissioned by the King to make a series of maps, and it was these maps that Alistair needed to uncover Comfry's hidden message. If Alistair was correct in his estimation, Sir Mirren would have, on hand, all of the maps necessary.

Finally the carriage rolled to a stop and Alistair exited the rig. The brick townhome was modest, reaching to three stories with a faded black door that boasted a brass number three on it. This was the address he had for Sir Mirren. He marched himself up the front steps to the stoop and slammed the brass knocker onto the door.

Several seconds passed and Alistair was beginning to think that no one was home, but then voices sounded from the other side of the door. He couldn't understand their words, but knew that more than one person spoke. Suddenly the door opened.

"How may I help y—" The words died on her lips as she looked up at him. "Alistair, er, my lord? How did you—? That is, why are you—? What are you doing here?"

"Winifred Wilmington." He let his eyes roam the length

of her. She looked the same, though perhaps more tempting with her face flushed from exertion. What precisely had she been doing behind that door only moments before? "I could ask you those same questions. I am here to see Sir Mirren."

She exhaled in one quick puff and opened the door wider. "Please come in."

He followed her inside and she led him to a door down the corridor on the left. As they entered the room, it was quite evident that this was Sir Mirren's study. That didn't explain what Winifred was doing here. He hadn't seen her in…it had to have been six years, since that fateful Christmas Eve he'd found her stranded in her carriage, trapped in the snow. They'd spent several days locked in his castle making love. And then—after the snow melted, making travel safe once more—she'd left and he'd never heard from her again. Which suited him just fine since he had no room in his life for females. Not since Sarah.

She sat behind the desk and motioned for him to sit adjacent to her.

"There is no delicate way to say this. I'm afraid Sir Mirren is dead," she said abruptly.

He frowned and tapped his cane against his boot. "I am sorry to hear that. Were you related to Mirren in some capacity?"

"I am his widow." She looked down at her dress, then blushed. "I know it is dreadful that I am not still in mourning, but there are extraneous circumstances." Her brow furrowed and it was then that he noticed she did look somewhat different. Delicate lines fanned from her eyes. "Is there something I can help you with?"

"Married? To Mirren? Since when?"

She chewed at her lip and her brows rose. "Since shortly after we met, actually."

She'd quite obviously had been engaged to marry Mirren

when she'd had her affair with him. "I thought you had been left at the altar."

"I was. My union with Reggie occurred after we met, my lord. He and I had been friends for a while and a marriage seemed a logical conclusion to our relationship."

She wasn't at all the woman he'd thought her to be—impulsive, passionate. No, this woman before him spoke of practicality. Not at all the Winifred who had invited herself into his bed. The woman who had taken refuge in his castle, in his arms, had been bold, refreshing—he shook his head, unable to reconcile the Winifred he'd bedded to the woman looking at him.

Well, none of that mattered now. He had other concerns at hand. "I need use of your husband's maps."

"His collection of maps is quite extensive. Perhaps you could narrow the selection for me?"

"I don't see why that is necessary."

Her eyes darted to the door behind him, then back to him. "If you could tell me which maps specifically you need to see, then perhaps I could locate them and have them brought to you."

"Your husband had hundreds upon hundreds of maps. You couldn't possibly search through them and find the ones I need."

Her posture stiffened, and her eyes narrowed in a glare. "Rest assured I am certainly capable of doing so. And I am certainly more familiar with my husband's collection than you are."

"Don't be ridiculous. It would take you days to sort—"

She stood, her glare intensified. "So now I am ridiculous?"

Somehow they had ended up in an argument. If people would simply concede to his requests, these sorts of fruitless battles would not ensue. She had no reason to be irritated with him.

"A man I barely know comes to my home, insults me, and demands to paw through my late husband's belongings, and you find me ridiculous?"

"I merely didn't want to inconvenience you. It makes far more sense for me to do it as I know what I'm looking for. There is truly no reason for you to get involved."

A door sounded in the corridor, then voices, followed by a childish giggle. Winifred came around the desk. "I don't see how I could grant you permission. Good day to you, my lord." She walked as if to leave the room.

He grabbed her arm as she passed him. "Winifred, it is of utmost importance that I have access to those maps." His form towered over her slighter one. She'd grown fuller over the years, and the curves did lovely things to her body. She was still a most handsome woman. He pulled her closer.

She swallowed visibly, her gaze darting to his mouth.

"I shall consider it, but you must be forthcoming with me," she said.

"The way you have been with me?" he asked before he thought better of it. Had he expected her to send him an invitation to her nuptials? "My apologies, it is not my concern whom you married."

An expression clouded her features, an emotion he did not recognize. Fear, perhaps, though her jaw was clearly set with stubbornness. "I shall consider it. I shall send notice to your address and let you know what I've decided." And then she disappeared out of the room.

Damnation. He was a spy. An elite spy, at that. He would not be outmaneuvered by a woman, no matter how alluring her curves. By the time that Alistair entered the corridor, it was empty of people. He was tempted to return to the study and search for the damn maps himself, but he'd been in the room long enough to know that unless there was a hidden compartment in there, the maps were elsewhere in this townhome.

Once in his carriage, he sat for several moments before directing the driver to his club. Perhaps it was time to make some inquiries as to Sir Mirren's widow. Again he was struck by the oddity of Winifred and Mirren's union. If he didn't know better, he'd think he was angry about how she'd returned to London fresh from his bed and rather quickly aligned herself with the mapmaker. But the fact was he didn't get angry with other people. Anger required a certain amount of emotion and he didn't care about people that much. And he didn't understand why most of them spent so much of their time wallowing in their own shallow emotions.

That was why he didn't like to deal with people. They were so damn inconvenient. And illogical. Despite his reputation, he was most definitely not a murderer, but there were times when he was glad that most of his life was spent in isolation.

• • •

Winifred must have turned eight shades of blue, she'd been so nervous. Good heavens, when she'd opened the door, she hadn't expected to find Alistair on the other side. She'd have been less surprised had the Reaper himself been there, hand outstretched, waiting to pull her into the beyond. But it had been Alistair. Thankfully Oliver hadn't been home at the moment; though when he'd arrived with his governess and had giggled in the corridor, she'd thought that Alistair would question her. But he hadn't seemed to notice, or care. Still, it was unsettling that Alistair had found her even if he'd been looking for Reggie instead.

Gracious, Alistair hadn't changed a bit. He was impossibly dashing and she'd wanted nothing more than to melt into him when he'd pulled her close. She'd scarcely been able to breathe, simultaneously worried he'd kiss her and worried he wouldn't.

Granting him access to Reggie's maps would have him in her home, as they were simply too large for her to transport. That, in turn, would put him near her son, and that simply could not happen. There had to be another way. Perhaps she could merely have him come when Oliver was out with his governess, in the park feeding the ducks. But how often could a boy feed ducks?

Of course, she could always tell Alistair the truth. How many letters had she written him over the years explaining precisely what had happened? She'd kept them all in a box under her bed. But she knew she couldn't tell him. He'd made it abundantly clear six years ago that he had no intention of ever marrying again, nor fathering a child. He'd even taken precautions with her, but obviously they hadn't been successful. He didn't want Oliver, and Reggie had kindly given the boy a name so no one need know the truth.

But how could she stand to be around Alistair and keep that secret? She'd never been a very good liar. That little voice inside her questioned her motive. It was the same voice that had convinced her to seduce Alistair in the first place, so she wasn't certain there was merit to the argument. Still, was Oliver the only reason she didn't want to be around Alistair, or did it go further than that? Was she afraid to be around him because she knew that once she granted him entrance to her life again, it was only a matter of time before she invited him to her bed?

She was simply going to have to turn down his request.

Chapter Two

Alistair once again entered Mirren's townhome, only this time he knew he waited for Winifred and not the deceased mapmaker. She came into the corridor in a huff, her face flushed, her breath winded. An image of her beneath him with the same expression came to his mind. The way she'd clung to him, cried out his name. No woman had ever responded to his touch the way Winifred had.

How had he managed to stay away from her for so many years?

"Good morning, Winifred."

"What are you doing here?"

"Did I interrupt anything?" He allowed his eyes to slowly slide down her form.

She wrapped her arms around her middle. "What I was doing is of no concern to you. I believe I told you yesterday that I would send word for you when I'd made my decision." She did not invite him into any other room; instead they stood in the main corridor.

"Indeed you did, but I believe that my presence here

will have more of the desired effect." He closed the distance between them and reached to finger a curl that had loosened by her ear. "Do you recall how I told you once that I tend to get what I want?"

She stared up into his eyes and she almost looked convinced, but then she swatted away his hand.

"Winnie, dear, what will it take to convince you that I need access to those maps?" he asked.

"Do not call me that. Reggie's cousin calls me that and I simply despise it."

"Do you prefer Fred?"

"No, I'd prefer you go away."

"Why the hostility?" He placed his hand on her upper arm, not to hold her there, but not quite a caress, either. "I seem to recall you enjoying my presence quite a bit. I also seem to recall you requesting my presence, as it were."

She pulled free from him and took several steps away. "Yes, well, that was a long time ago." She patted her hair. "Tell me why you need the maps."

"That I cannot do."

"Cannot or will not?"

"Does it matter?" How was it possible she could simultaneously be charming and annoying?

"Yes, it does. One implies that you do not wish to share the information with me. The other implies that you cannot tell anyone."

"If you recall, I work for the Crown," he said. "That is all I can say."

"So this is business with the war department," she said. "Interesting." She was quiet for several moments. "Though I've been through all of Reggie's maps and I can assure you he was harboring no secrets that would benefit England. In fact, the majority of his maps were commissioned by King George himself."

"I believe I shall be the judge of what is and isn't beneficial." He stepped closer to her, and she backed up until her body was pressed against the wood paneling lining the wall behind her. This close, he could smell the lemon oil the servants used to polish the wood, but even that could not cover Winifred's scent of spices and cloves. He inhaled.

Her eyes narrowed at him. "So I'm supposed to simply allow you access to my personal belongings simply because you work for the Crown?" she asked.

"Precisely." When she still had not budged, he added, "These are maps. It is not as if I am asking to rifle through your corsets and chemises."

She crossed her arms over her chest and pink stained her cheeks. "Be that as it may, I shall need more persuading than that."

He once again fingered the curl by her ear. "It shall be my pleasure." He braced his hands on either side of her and leaned in close. "I've never forgotten you, you know. Those few nights you spent in my bed. Men do not forget women with such passion, such eagerness."

Her breath hitched. "I've changed."

"Pity." He leaned in closer and nuzzled her ear. "Do you remember how you would cry out my name? Again and again." He kissed the pulse that flickered in her neck.

She said nothing.

"I remember this smell, the way you rinse your hair with cloves. You smell exotic, do you know that? Like some goddess from the pages of Homer's *Iliad*." He kissed her throat again. "I still remember how to touch you to make you cry out, to make you beg me to make love to you."

"I told you, I've changed. I'm a widow." Her words were strong, but her tone weak and unconvincing.

"Am I to believe that Reginald Mirren, the old mapmaker"—he traced a finger across her collarbone—"was such a good lover that you will not respond to my touch anymore?"

She shivered in spite of herself. "I shall not discuss my marriage with you."

He took her earlobe in his teeth and nibbled. Licked the outer edge of her ear.

She sucked in a breath and he would have sworn she leaned into him.

He had not come here to seduce her, but damned if Winifred wasn't tempting. He didn't crave contact with other people, but he was still a man, and certainly still had urges, though normally he could keep them in check. Had she not come into the room with mussed hair and flushed cheeks, he might not have remembered how it had felt to lose himself inside of her willing body. No, that was a lie. He'd never forget her willing body.

He was hard, and he wanted her, right here up against this wall. He moved his lips to her mouth and kissed her, gently, sweetly, as if only to remind himself of her taste. But it wasn't enough. He coaxed her mouth open with his tongue, and it took little persuasion on his part before she was kissing him back. Her hands thread through his hair, pulling him down to her.

Damnation, but he'd missed her.

With her body pressed so close to his, she couldn't possibly miss his arousal, so he pressed it against her.

She clung to him, kissed him, as if she, too, needed him for survival. He brought his hand up and cupped her breast. She arched against him and he knew that he could have her, right in the grand foyer of her late husband's townhome. But he hadn't come for her. And she'd never agree to give him access to those maps if he seduced her right now.

So with more strength than he realized he had, he ended the kiss and stepped away from her.

"I shall return tomorrow to see if you've made your decision about the maps. Good day to you." And with that he walked away.

•••

What the devil had that been? Her breaths were still shaky. She shook her hands out and concentrated on her inhalations and exhalations.

She'd been nearly ready to pull up her dress and wrap her legs around his body. She had to find some control or at least enough strength to pretend she had control. Though it seemed as if she had virtually none when it came to Alistair Devlin. If he weren't so ridiculously handsome and such a scandalously good kisser… She sighed and sagged against the wall.

"Never thought we'd see the likes of him again," Polly said.

Winifred jumped. "Polly! I've told you a million times not to sneak up on me."

"Lost in your thoughts or merely thinking about that kiss?"

"That"—she pointed at her maid—"is none of your concern. How long were you standing there watching?"

Polly shrugged. "Long enough."

Winifred merely released a low breath. It would do no good to chastise Polly. Although she was technically an employee, they were more like family. "Have I sacked you yet this week?"

"Not yet," she said with a mocking grin. "Are you going to give him what he wants?"

"I—"

Polly held up one hand. "The maps. I don't want to know about anything else."

"I'm not certain I have a choice. It seems as if he will merely continue stopping by until I give in."

"If you'll have to give in no matter what, you might as well get something out of it in exchange."

"I don't need anything. Our finances are secure."

"All I'm saying is a man with his name could be useful."

Before Winifred could disagree, she knew precisely what Alistair could do for her. "You're brilliant, Polly." She kissed her maid on the cheek and ran out of the corridor. She had to carefully plan how she would strike such a bargain with Alistair. If she wasn't careful, he'd be wagering how long it would take him to get her back into his bed.

It had been too long since her body had felt such things.

She and Reggie had never consummated their marriage. Not because she hadn't been willing—she'd taken her marital responsibilities to heart. They'd tried, but Reggie had problems with impotency. She'd wondered if it was her fault, if there had been something wrong with her that she couldn't please her husband, but Reggie had assured her that it had far more to do with his advancing years.

Bless his sweet heart, he'd loved her. Loved her in a way she'd never loved him. And he'd loved her son. Reggie had been a wonderful man and she'd been blessed to have spent time as his wife. Not many of her friends could say the same about their husbands. Nor could they say they'd had illicit affairs and a bastard son with the Marquess of Coventry. Her body still hummed with desire and she knew she'd have to be strong when she saw him again.

Having a bargain of her own would prevent him from trying to seduce her into granting him access to the maps. Which was perfect because the more he kissed her, the more she wanted things she knew she could not have. Because no matter what, there was no future for her with Alistair.

Chapter Three

Winifred pulled Oliver closer to her and turned the page. It was his favorite story and he asked her to read it to him at least once a week, which she cheerfully indulged. Well, he asked in his way, by crawling up beside her on the settee while holding the book. He was five years old and she had yet to hear him utter a single word. She tried to not let that concern her overly much, but the truth was, it was rather distressing that Oliver remained so wordless.

She knew he wasn't a simpleton. He was quite intelligent, actually. He'd proven that recently when she'd left a ledger out where she'd been working on calculations. She'd gone to retrieve something and when she'd returned, Oliver had completed the mathematics. Perfectly.

He giggled at a particular part where she used a funny voice to characterize a character. She wiggled her fingers into his side and he giggled all the more. Oh, how she loved him.

A slight rap came at the door, then Polly entered. "He's here again."

Winifred's heart pounded. "Lord Coventry? He was only

here a few hours ago." So far his visits had occurred while Oliver had been out of the house or otherwise occupied, which worked perfectly because one look at the boy and he would know who the father was.

"No, ma'am, it's the Virgil man."

"Ah yes," She had forgotten it was about time for Reggie's cousin's weekly visit.

"He wishes to see you first before he sees the boy," Polly said.

"We shall have to finish this later, my love." She kissed Oliver's head and ruffled his brown hair. "Polly, bring him down in ten minutes. No longer."

"Yes, ma'am."

Winifred straightened her dress and made her way down the stairs to the study where she knew she'd find Virgil. He was officially the legal guardian for Oliver, though he allowed the boy to stay with his mother. She was thankful for that, but not much else when it came to Virgil. She didn't trust him, but she knew that Reggie had had no other choice when deciding upon a will. He'd had to name a male relative as Oliver's guardian. Virgil could legally make most of the decisions for Oliver, and she hated that.

She entered the study and found him standing behind the desk as if he belonged there. He wore a ridiculously offensive blue velvet coat and striped breeches and his reddish hair was oiled back flat on his head. He was woefully thin and his sartorial choices gave him an awkward, bird-like appearance. She'd often thought he looked quite like a turkey. "My dear Winnie," he said as she approached.

She winced at the nickname. "Virgil." She inclined her head. "You wished to speak to me privately?"

"Yes, I've been considering your situation and I believe I have struck on a solution."

"My situation?" She wasn't aware they'd discussed

anything of the sort before, so the fact that he'd found a solution for her was surprising.

He waved his hand as if the motion would explain his words. "Yes, yes, being a widow. And having the young boy, Arthur."

"Oliver," she corrected.

"Yes, yes, that's right." He moved from behind the desk, trailed his hand along the books on the shelf. "You need to find yourself a new husband."

"Oh, I don't believe that is necessary. Though I am not against marrying again, I'm not in any hurry to do so. I'm only just out of mourning." She moved behind one of the chairs, somehow feeling better with furniture placed between them.

"But there could be a hurry. You see all of those funds that Arthur earns each month from the investments Reggie made for him."

"Oliver," she repeated. She resisted the urge to roll her eyes heavenward. How difficult was it, really, to remember one child's name?

"Right, well, they go into my coffers, but the will states that should you remarry, your new husband would receive them."

What was he suggesting? He had always been peculiar, but he was acting even more strangely than usual. "You are so eager to rid yourself of the extra coin?"

"On the contrary, I was suggesting a union between the two of us." He came to stand near her. She tried, in vain, not to stare at his beak-like nose. "I shall keep the earnings, but it would be official and therefore you could retain some of the funds from the property. I am merely thinking of you, Winnie dear, and what is best for you and the boy."

"I'm sorry, did you just propose marriage to me?"

He took a few steps even closer and she was struck by how very thin his legs were. Frankly it was astounding he could walk upright. "I did. It's a perfect solution for both of us."

She narrowed her eyes at him. "I don't see how." More than likely he knew about *her* coffers, the money that she'd brought into the marriage that Reggie had allowed her to keep in her name only. And that was what Virgil was truly after, a sum far greater than Reggie's investments would bring. Perhaps Virgil was not a turkey, but rather a vulture.

"You are a widow now, and it is unsafe for a single woman to be raising a child alone."

"I am perfectly safe. Thank you for your concern."

"Marry me, Winnie," he said.

"I'd really rather not. But I do appreciate the offer."

"Let me put it in terms you shall understand. Marry me and I won't send your boy off to boarding school." His brows rose.

"Are you threatening me?"

"Of course not." He gave his head a slight shake. "I'm merely giving you a choice."

She frowned, not bothering to temper her reaction. "It sounds more like an ultimatum."

"I cannot be certain of the choices that some other man would make for the dear boy and I cannot allow that to happen. My cousin entrusted his well-being to me."

"So if I do not marry you?"

He grinned and she realized that Virgil was missing more than one tooth. She shuddered. "Then I do believe I have found a perfect school for him," he said. "Somewhere quite far away."

Winifred could feel her nostrils flaring and she knew that if she was not careful, she would say something she very much regretted. "I should like some time to think on this."

"Of course. Not too much time, though." He glanced at the clock on the mantle. "No time to see the boy today. I'll be back. Be ready with your answer."

She watched him leave and realized that Alistair's reappearance in her life could not only assist with Oliver's tutor situation, but with Virgil as well. Now it seemed the only thing left in question was how badly Alistair needed those maps.

· · ·

Alistair stood outside the door to his study, listening to the woman's voice from inside the room.

"Yes, I shall agree to you viewing the maps, but you must do something for me in exchange." Then, "No, no, that's not right. Let's see. I shall grant your petition, but you shall grant one of mine." There were several low mutterings. "Why are you so addled, you silly girl?"

He'd known she'd eventually agree to his petition. He chose that moment to step inside. "Yes, why are you so addled?"

Her cheeks stained with red and she opened her mouth, then closed it. A frown furrowed her brow and he was struck again by how delightfully expressive she was.

"How much did you hear?" she asked.

"Enough to know you want an exchange of favors, so to speak." He walked over to the center of the room and took a seat in the large brown leather chair. He motioned to one of the other chairs. "Sit, we can discuss the parameters."

She exhaled loudly, but nonetheless took a seat.

"What is it that I can do for you, sweet Winifred?"

She fiddled with her gloves, pinching the bits of the fabric that stuck out from her fingertips. "Yes, well, it would seem I'm in need of a tutor. A specific tutor and he will not return any of my letters."

"A tutor? Precisely what do you need a tutor for? Are

you not already educated?"

"Of course I am. This is for my son." She looked up at him. "Yes, I have a son. And he is in need of some precise tutoring, but as I said, the man will not respond."

A child. He had not anticipated that, though it stood to reason. She'd been married. Most men wanted an heir to carry on their name. *Most men.* "And you are set on this particular tutor?"

"Oh yes, he has the very best of reputations, but he is quite difficult to employ. But certainly a man with your title could implore him to accept the position."

"Do you have the necessary funds?"

Again she fidgeted with her gloves. "Yes, I do. My own personal monies that I received when my parents died."

"And Mirren's money?"

"Tied up with my son and his guardian." She shrugged.

"And this guardian cannot provide the same service you believe I can?"

She exhaled slowly. "No, he can provide nothing for me. In this situation or any other. In fact, he has suggested that I marry him. Threatened me, actually." Her eyes widened. "I shouldn't have said any of that. I meant only that he doesn't provide the same kind of reputation and name that you can when persuading this particular tutor."

"He is threatening you?"

"That is truly not the point."

It most certainly seemed the point. His fists clenched. He was not accustomed to feeling the need to protect someone, but the emotion was unmistakable.

"Will you contact this man for me, implore him to accept my son as a student?"

"Do you have other children?" He couldn't deny that he found the whole idea of her carrying Mirren's child rather irritating.

"No, only the one." She smoothed her hands down her skirt.

"Very well. If I do this for you, you shall grant me access to Mirren's maps?"

"Yes, if you convince this tutor to agree to work with me, the maps are at your disposal."

He inclined his head. "I'll need the man's name and address." He stood and retrieved a piece of parchment and quill. "Write them down."

She did as he instructed and then met his gaze.

"You have surprised me today, Winifred. I was not expecting you to be a mother."

"Why?" she asked, her tone bristled. "Do you not think I am qualified to be a mother?"

"I'm certain I know many things about you, but whether or not you are skilled as a mother, I cannot say."

"There is one other tiny matter, of which you could be helpful," she said.

"More favors? What have you been doing for so long without me in your life?"

"Yes, well, perhaps our little reunion is merely good timing." She smoothed her skirts though there was not a wrinkle in sight. "In any case. The aforementioned guardian who wishes to marry me. I believe it might be a deterrent if he thinks I am connected to another man. A man of your station."

He wasn't quite believing her words. He'd told her years ago that he wasn't interested in marrying again. "You want me to marry you?"

She frowned, shook her head. "Of course not. I merely want you to pretend you are going to marry me. At least until he loses interest in me as a prospect."

"What would this charade entail?" he asked.

"Nothing more than me being able to tell him about our

pending nuptials. Perhaps he could meet you, too. You are formidable. I suspect if he saw you, he would lose interest in me rather quickly."

"Formidable." He nodded. "And these are your conditions for allowing me access to the maps?"

"Yes."

"Very well."

She stood to leave, clutching her bag against her stomach.

"Leaving so soon? You could join me for tea," he suggested. He picked up the bell to ring it.

"That won't be necessary."

He moved closer to her. "I can't help but notice that you seem nervous around me."

She swallowed. "Of course not. Why would I be nervous?" But before he could answer, she continued, "I merely have another appointment. Please let me know as soon as you have made arrangements with Mr. Bellford."

He nodded. But he knew that Winifred was, indeed, anxious about something, and it bothered him. Normally he found no interest in the emotions of others, as most people seemed to advance from one feeling to the next rather rapidly. Winifred was different, though, and that in and of itself was a problem.

Chapter Four

The following day, Alistair was waiting for her in her study just as she assumed he would be. The man was nothing if not prompt. Not to mention persistent. She'd already received notice from Mr. Bellford that he'd be by to meet her son tomorrow at three. She was relieved and thrilled that the man had finally agreed to meet with Oliver. But she couldn't pretend she wasn't also equally annoyed. She had sent the man no fewer than ten requests and all it had taken was one from Alistair. But that was the way things were with men.

Though he did not require her assistance with the maps, she'd already decided she would stay with him while he worked. It would ensure he stayed away from Oliver and perhaps clue her into what he was working on. She couldn't deny her own curiosity.

She walked past the looking glass in the second floor corridor, then backed up to stand before it. She took a look at herself, then rolled her eyes at her frivolity and walked away. It mattered not what she looked like. This was a business agreement and nothing more. Besides, she knew she looked differently than she had six years ago. Her body was fuller from having Oliver, and some of the extra weight still clung to her curves. She had changed in other ways since becoming a mother. She was no longer that impulsive, carefree girl Alistair had rescued. In many ways, he knew her as no one else ever had, not simply because she'd given him her body, but because she had been free with him in a way she'd never been with anyone else.

She caught herself before she patted her hair, then she stepped into Reggie's former study.

"Alistair," she said. Why was it that the room felt twice as large when she had to cross it in front of him? The back of her neck warmed as if she could feel his eyes on her. But it would do no good to allow him to see his affect on her.

"Now then, do you know precisely which maps you need?" she asked once she stood behind Reggie's old desk.

"All of them," he said, his voice deep and sensual, which was ridiculous because nothing he had said was in the least bit sensual.

"All of them? I'm certain you can be more specific."

"I need to see them to know precisely which ones I need. They are named, no?"

He was bound and determined to be difficult about the matter. But he'd done her a substantial favor and secured a tutor she'd been trying to contact for the better part of a year. She would have to grant him some concessions. "Yes, they are named. Very well, come this way."

"To where, precisely?"

"The map room, of course."

"Of course," he said drolly.

He silently followed her down the corridor to the back of the house. Reggie's map room had two windows, but they were always shrouded with draperies so that the maps would not fade in the sunlight. Winifred lit the lanterns and soft, gold light illuminated the room.

She still came in here on occasion, when she was missing her sweet husband, the man who had loved her and had been satisfied that she had not loved him in return. He'd been a true friend to her and she would miss him always.

For the most part, though, this room had gone untouched since Reggie had died, nearly fourteen months before. A long mahogany table stretched across one side of the room and several maps lay unrolled and held down with various glass bobs. The rest of the maps resided in a cabinet Reggie had commissioned many years before.

"We can use this table," she said.

"We?" he asked, brows raised.

"Yes, I shall be assisting you."

"I don't require assistance."

"Perhaps not, but you require me for access to these maps." She gave him a deliberately sweet smile, which he seemed totally immune to.

It was the one thing that perplexed her most about Alistair. How could he evoke such emotions from her yet seem to feel none of his own? It was a mystery...he was a mystery.

He stepped over to the table and glanced at the maps.

"The rest are here?" he asked, indicating the cabinet behind him.

"Yes."

He said nothing more, but merely sat and withdrew a small bound book from the inside of his coat. He opened it and read silently. Then he looked back at the maps. "No, no, and no." He walked over to peruse the maps in the cabinet.

She watched his methodical movements. He'd unroll a map, glance over it, and either make a note in a second notebook or return the map to its previous place.

He seemed to not be bothered by her presence, nor did

he attempt to include her in his work. After an hour, he set down his quill and met her gaze.

"I should like to have an affair with you."

"I beg your pardon?" Her heart thundered in her ears.

"We are well suited in the bedroom, if you recall. And we are both unattached now. You certainly have no need to be concerned of your reputation. Not that you ever were. It is logical."

She frowned and felt the weight of her brow as it furrowed above her eyes. "I don't believe logic plays a part in matters of the heart."

"I am not speaking of the heart. Merely of a carnal relationship. As we had before, as you once suggested."

He tossed her own words back at her and she winced.

"I know you still feel desire toward me. I felt that in your kiss yesterday."

Winifred stared openly at him. He was quite serious, she knew that. Alistair was not one for jests. In fact, she wasn't altogether certain he had a sense of humor. She ignored her body's reaction to his shocking request. She wanted him, and the mere glance of his eyes lingering at her cleavage had her breathing short. The desire was there, and of course Alistair knew. He'd always been able to see that in her.

Finally, he nodded. "You obviously need time to consider."

"Alistair, we cannot have an affair."

"Of course we can. If we can pretend to be betrothed, we can have an affair."

"It is not that simple."

"It is actually quite simple." He gathered his materials and stood. "I believe you know where I reside. We shall dine tonight at eight."

That was the extent of his invitation. If she wanted something more romantic, she would never get it from him.

"I shall see you out," she said.

"I know my way out. Until tonight, Winifred."

Did he mean to start an affair with her tonight? At his townhome? After they dined on pheasant and boiled potatoes? Gracious, having Alistair back in her life had most assuredly complicated things rather quickly.

. . .

Alistair had meant to propose the affair with more finesse, but he never had been good at those sorts of things. Hell, when he and Sarah had gotten betrothed, he'd simply looked at her and said, "Our parents said we're a good match." And he'd left it at that. Of course their parents had been the only reason they'd married in the first place.

Now Winifred was coming to dinner. If he were a gentleman, he'd propose marriage and not a carnal affair. But he wasn't good at marriage and he knew he could never provide the things Winifred would need. He'd never been good with people, and he suspected he'd be even worse with children, so he couldn't offer her a new life. But he could offer her pleasure.

He found he not only craved physical touch, but *her* physical touch. An affair was the perfect solution. But that would not solve her problem with her son's guardian. For that, Alistair would need to pay the man a visit.

Doing so should eliminate the man's interest in Winifred. She'd assured Alistair that this guardian was only after money, and she had no interest in pursuing a relationship with him. If she didn't want the man and he'd expressed no interest in her son outside the financials, then it was time the man was convinced his attentions were required elsewhere.

As his carriage rolled to a stop outside of Reginald Mirren's cousin's home, Alistair planned what he'd tell the man. He was inclined to merely threaten him, but perhaps he would start with logic and see where that led him.

He rapped on the door with his cane and waited. Several minutes later a wizened housekeeper came to the door. She looked up at him, and her thin, white brows rose. "Yes?"

"I need to see Mr. Mirren." He handed her his calling card.

Her eyes widened. "Come in, my lord." She led him to a tiny parlor at the front of the house. The furniture was faded but well kept. She left him, and not a minute later, his host entered the room.

"My lord," Virgil said with an exaggerated bow. "To what do I owe this visit?"

Alistair realized instantly that what little money this bloke had, he spent entirely on clothing. His embroidered green coat hung perfectly over the man's purple and green striped breeches. If all it would take was money...

"We have a friend in common," Alistair said.

"Indeed? Who is it?" Virgil took a seat, but looked so ill at ease, he appeared as if he'd jump up from his chair at any moment.

"Mrs. Winifred Mirren, your cousin's late wife."

"Ah, sweet Winnie. She's a delight, is she not?"

"She is to marry me. I shall see to it that you are paid handsomely for staying out of her and her son's life. Should they require your assistance, I'm certain Winifred"—he emphasized her full Christian name—"would know how to reach you."

"I was not aware that Winifred had another suitor." Virgil's features pinched. "How handsomely?"

"We can start with three thousand pounds, and if I am pleased with your absence, then perhaps you shall see more." Alistair stood to his full height and tapped his cane on the wood floor. "But I will not hesitate to return here should the situation arise."

"Three thousand pounds, that is quite generous." He stood and eagerly pumped Alistair's hand in an entirely too friendly handshake. "I can see now that you will be able to care for Winifred and her son in a way that I cannot. Obviously she is better suited with you." *Well suited.* That's what everyone had said about him and Sarah. But their union had been a disaster. Alistair forced the thought from his mind and instructed Virgil that the monies would be delivered by the end of the week. He could only imagine what audacious clothing the man would purchase with that much coin in his pocket.

Informing Winifred that she need not concern herself with Virgil any longer should aid in Alistair's campaign to seduce her back into his bed.

• • •

Winifred knew that if she did not accept Alistair's invite to accompany him for dinner, he would merely continue pestering her until she did. Oliver had already gone to bed, and Winifred had left Polly to care for him should he wake up.

So she sat in the carriage outside of his illustrious townhome in the center of Mayfair on Charles Street. There had been a time shortly after their brief affair that she'd fancied herself in love with Alistair. He was so different from any man she'd ever known, and though she didn't always understand it, she was drawn to him.

And now he'd proposed another affair. She couldn't deny that she was tempted to accept. The thought of being in his arms again made a very compelling argument. But considering she'd nearly had her heart broken the last time, she wasn't certain it was worth it. Not only that, but there was

Oliver to consider.

Alistair had never wanted children, and he'd made that perfectly clear when they'd had their affair at his castle.

A knock sounded on the carriage door. She started at the sound, but opened it and found a footman standing there.

"His lordship would like to know if you're planning on coming inside."

She should have known he'd be watching. "Yes, of course." She allowed the man to help her down and lead her up the stairs to the front door.

"He said you should wait in the parlor."

When Alistair did not enter the room immediately, Winifred strolled to the bookshelf to read the titles of his books. His townhome, much like his castle, was opulent without being ostentatious.

"You are beautiful." Alistair's words came from directly behind her. He stated the compliment as if it were a fact, rather than merely his opinion.

How had she not heard him approach, felt his nearness? She turned to find his intense green eyes upon her. "Thank you."

"I don't think you understand how beautiful."

"You're not normally one for flattery, Alistair."

"Merely curious. You could have married anyone, yet you were jilted once and then ended up married to an aged mapmaker."

His words stung, though she knew he didn't mean them to be hurtful. "Do you have a particular question, or are you only interested in questioning my decisions?"

"Why Mirren?"

She shrugged. "He asked."

"So you would have agreed to anyone's request of your hand?"

"Of course not." The situation hadn't been simple at all.

Reggie had known she'd found herself with child and he'd saved her and her son, given them both a name and no one had been the wiser. She certainly couldn't tell Alistair that.

He nodded. "Are you hungry?"

Thankful the uncomfortable conversation had ended, she smiled. "I suppose I am."

Besides, it was far better to have a table between them than this empty space. Too much temptation to give in to his earlier request.

He held his arm out to her and she took it, his gloved hand resting on hers in the crook of his elbow as he led her into the dining room. The table was ridiculously large for simply the two of them, but was a beautiful carved mahogany. The places were set next to one another, Alistair's at the head and hers to his right.

"What are we having? It smells delicious."

"I haven't a notion. I leave the meals up to the cook's choices. I shall eat whatever is prepared." He looked up at her after taking his seat. "Are you a choosy eater?"

"Not normally. I'm certain whatever it is will be delightful."

A footman served their first dish and the steaming, aromatic parsnip soup caused her stomach to grumble. She waited for Alistair to pick up his spoon before doing so herself and took a small spoonful.

"I spoke with your son's guardian today. I don't believe he'll be bothering you about marriage again," he said.

Her breath caught. The thought of Alistair telling that vile man that she was to marry the marquess instead—well, it was liberating. "You saw Virgil? How did you find him?"

"I am not without my resources."

"What did you say?"

"It was quite evident to me that while the man obviously values money, he has none—"

"You paid him?" she asked.

"Quite handsomely. He should leave you alone and only tend to his duties as the boy's guardian. Though I doubt he'll do much of that either, outside of signing any papers required of him."

After a moment, she realized she'd been staring at him, mouth agape. "Alistair, I did not ask you to pay him." Then she suppressed a giggle. "I do wonder why I never thought of that myself. Would you allow me to pay you back the funds?"

"I'm tempted as I know all he's going to do is purchase more clothes." Alistair rolled his eyes heavenward. "He dresses ridiculously."

To that she laughed; a full belly laugh.

"But no, I do not require you to pay me in return."

"Thank you."

He nodded. "Have you given more consideration to my offer this afternoon?"

"The affair," she said, plainly knowing that attempting to feign stupidity would not work with Alistair. "I do not think it is a good idea."

"That is not an answer."

"No, it isn't." She set down her spoon. "Is this why you invited me to dinner tonight? To seduce me into an affair?"

"I don't believe seduction is required. We both want each other. There is no need to play games. It is as simple as this food." He motioned to the plate before him. "We are hungry, therefore we have food."

Winifred laughed. Alistair certainly had a unique perspective on things. "Tell me what you have done with yourself these last several years."

He eyed her for a while, saying nothing, before he said, "Working mostly. Keeping to myself."

"Staying in the country tucked away in your castle?"

"I prefer the quiet of the countryside to the noise of

London. There are too many people here." He'd said the latter with so much unpleasantness, it was as if he was commenting on the number of spiders.

She couldn't argue with his sentiment, though. While she didn't find people as tedious as he did, she had found London's population increase as of late to be somewhat overwhelming. Shopping excursions had become a chore with the crowded sidewalks. London was positively bursting with people.

They finished their dinner and he led her into a parlor off of the dining room. He took a seat on the settee. "Sit with me."

She did as he suggested, but left space between them. As it was, she was already far too tempted to indulge in the affair he'd proposed. When she'd been at his castle, they'd spoken briefly of his work for the Crown. He'd told her only that he deciphered codes, nothing specific. "Have you worked on anything of interest?"

"My work is always of interest, or else why would I do it?"

"What is it that makes it so compelling?"

"I enjoy the puzzles." He slid across the settee, bringing them closer. "You are presenting quite the puzzle at the moment."

"How so?"

He toyed with one of the curls at the nape of her neck. The light touch was as intoxicating as if he'd caressed her. "You want me and I obviously desire you as well, yet you're being rather illogical about the situation."

"I suspect it's quite fascinating, the work you do," she said, ignoring his last statement. "Are there many codes for you to decipher?"

Perhaps she wouldn't engage his proposition because she knew she had no legitimate argument to stand on. Perhaps it was because she was too nervous. She simply didn't want to be swept away. She didn't want wild, raging, out of control passion that would leave her cold and empty when he inevitably left her.

Yes, she wanted him. Wanted his heat without getting burned. Wanted his body without losing her heart.

She sucked in a long, deep breath, trying to still the nerves in her hands, trying to squelch her desire. She should leave. She should stand and walk away from him.

He ran a fingertip down the back of her neck. His finger was hot, searing her sensitive skin. Then she felt his lips touch the back of her neck. The moist pressure of his mouth against the delicate skin just below her ear. The tender nip of his teeth.

She shivered. No nerves this time. Just pleasure. Her eyes closed and she leaned into him. Heat swirled through her, the desire pooling in the folds of her femininity. His mouth was at her ear, murmuring to her—how her beauty had only grown with time and how he'd never forgotten the taste of her kiss. The tone of his voice, deep and seductive, rumbled through her. Oh, how she'd missed his voice.

Wistful longing thrummed through her, reminding her of how she'd missed him, all of him, and how difficult it had been to let her heart forget. With more strength than she knew she possessed, she put her hands on him and gently pushed.

"I can't do this."

Chapter Five

Two days later, they stood in the map room and Alistair paced from the table to the cabinet. Winifred watched him carefully. His movements were always precise, but today they were sharp, agitated.

"Do you know where the other maps are?" he asked.

"I might."

He braced his hands on the table and set his eyes on her. "Winifred, do not play games with me."

She glared at him in return. "I am not playing games. And I should remind you, there is no need to talk to me in such a way. I realize that people indulge your abrasiveness because of your title, but I will not stand for it."

He nodded. "You're right. My apologies."

"I said I *think* I know where they are, but I cannot be certain."

"Explain."

She exhaled slowly. "A few years before Reggie died, he had an apprentice. A young man to whom he was teaching all of his methods and whatnot."

"I know what an apprentice is."

"Yes, well, Reggie and Timothy had a falling out, as it were, and Reggie terminated their association. Shortly after Reggie died, several of the maps that he and Timothy had worked on together went missing. I've always suspected Timothy took them, but figured if he needed them that badly, he should simply keep them."

"Do you know where we can find this Timothy?" Alistair asked.

"I have an address for him."

"I shall go and see him straightaway. I must have those maps."

"I doubt he will help you," she said.

"Why is that?"

"He's a peculiar sort, has ill feelings toward the aristocracy. I believe he was raised by his uncle, an earl, and then when he became of age, he was sent away to make his own way in the world."

"I don't care about any of that."

"I simply think he will be reluctant to speak with you." She wasn't even certain that she wanted to see him again. The last time she'd seen Timothy, he'd made her feel extremely uncomfortable.

"I will make him comply."

"What are you going to do, barge in there and shoot him if he doesn't agree to hand over the maps?"

"If I have to. This is business for the King."

She rolled her eyes. "Gracious, there is no need for dramatics. Timothy will help me. He has a soft spot where I'm concerned." She frowned. "Or he did at the time. But I do not wish to see him. Can we not simply send him a message?"

"No. Why do you not want to see him?"

"I am the reason Reggie dismissed him."

"You had an affair with him?"

"Of course not." She swatted him on the arm. "But he attempted to seduce me. On more than one occasion, he became too friendly with his hands." She searched Alistair's face. "Honestly, do you think I would enter an affair with just any man? Your perception of me is so flattering."

"I think most highly of you." His tone held no hint of jesting. "Certainly you must know that by now."

She nodded, but found she had no words to respond.

"A message will not work, but I shall accompany you and I will make certain this Timothy understands that you belong to me."

His words thundered through her heart and for the briefest of moments, she wished they were true. Wished that he had barged back into her life and demanded, not that they have an affair, but rather that she marry him. "How will you do that?"

"Tell him you are my betrothed."

Betrothed. Not wife. For Alistair, it was nothing but a charade.

• • •

Alistair had insisted on seeing Timothy that very day, and Winifred had done her best to look the part of fiancée to the illustrious Marquess of Coventry. She'd donned her prettiest dress and had Polly do up her hair nicely. Alistair had suggested they appear as if they were on their way to a soiree or dinner party to solidify their story of being romantically connected.

She took one last glance at the mirror and walked out of her bedchamber.

She had not conceded to his request for an affair. *Yet.* That word kept flitting through her mind as if the acquiescence was inevitable. She certainly was in a position in her life where she could have an affair. She was a widow, but she was also a mother, and that should count for more than anything. Especially more than her own baser desires.

She had to keep her focus on Oliver. Now that he had the

right tutor, he would be able to flourish. When her parents had died, they'd left her a rather large sum of monies and since then, she'd invested wisely and the monies had grown. When the time came, she'd be able to pay for Oliver to attend whatever school he desired.

But first Oliver had to start talking. She could barely contain her excitement that her son was finally working with Mr. Bellford. He'd come so highly recommended, especially with boys that had difficulties. And she needed someone who wouldn't give up on her son and believe him a simpleton simply because he never spoke. He was quite gifted, she'd ascertained, and she needed someone else to believe that, to see Oliver for who he was and help him to become a successful man.

He was so very like his father. She'd known that the moment they had placed him in her arms. He'd been born with a shock of brown hair and as he'd grown, his eyes had darkened to the same lovely green as Alistair's. One look and she was certain that Alistair would know the boy's lineage. Which was why it was so very important that they never meet.

Downstairs, Alistair waited for her in the corridor. He looked ridiculously dashing in buckskin breeches and black tailcoat. The flash of white at his throat with his expertly tied cravat highlighted his dark good looks.

"Alistair, I daresay, you are positively dashing this evening."

He gave her a rare grin and held his arm out to her. "You are beautiful as usual."

He assisted her into the carriage and they sat quietly next to one another while the rig rolled down the street. Warmth from his leg permeated the space between them, and she crossed her ankles to keep her legs tightly together. There was no need to act the wanton.

"If this man does not have the maps, have you any notion as to who else might have stolen them?" he asked.

"No, Timothy is the only man who would want them."

"That, I doubt."

"They're old maps. Unless we're talking a collector, there's no reason for someone to steal them."

"Someone has obviously seen them, or else they would not have been able to use them for the code I am working on. Are you acquainted with Lord Comfry?"

He had not told her as much, but she'd assumed he was working on something of the sort. She knew he worked for the Crown, did secretive assignments, and focused his talents on deciphering hidden messages and codes. But who could have possibly used Reggie's maps for such a thing? "I can't say that I've heard that name."

"Did Mirren ever have any other apprentices?"

"No, not in the time that we were together."

His frown deepened.

"Do you suspect Timothy of anything…inappropriate?" she asked.

"I couldn't say. And that's not my task. Once the code is broken, the others will decide what happens next."

He was so confident. Not *if* he broke the code, but once he'd done so. "Have you ever found a code you could not decipher?"

"No."

And I always get what I want. He didn't say it, but the words seemed to linger in the tiny confines of the carriage. She would be in his bed, in other words.

The carriage stopped outside a small boardinghouse. They walked up to the front door and an elderly lady opened it.

"What?" she asked sharply.

"We're looking for Mr. Timothy Drake. Tell him that Winifred Mirren is here to see him."

"Tell him yourself. Third door from the left, upstairs." The woman moved out of their way, then closed the door behind them.

The staircase creaked and moaned as they ascended.

"Allow me," Winifred said. She knocked on the third door and Alistair lingered off to the side.

When the door opened, Timothy grinned at the sight of her. "Finally changed your mind?" He reached out to grab her hand. "I knew you felt it, too, the pull between us. Oh, Winifred, I'm glad you—"

Alistair put his hand on her shoulder and stepped into view, and Timothy stopped talking.

Timothy looked up at the imposing man behind her. He swallowed visibly.

"May we come in?" she asked.

"Yes, of course," Timothy said.

It was a small room with three chairs, all different, sitting near the fireplace. A writing desk that had obviously seen better days stood in the corner.

"What can I do for you?" he asked.

"The maps, Timothy, where are they?"

He backed away, shrugging. "I don't know what you mean."

"The ones you stole from the house right after Reggie died. I know you took them."

Alistair said nothing, merely cleared his throat. It was enough of a threat for the boy to nod.

"I needed the money."

"You sold them?" Alistair asked.

"I had to. I had nothing."

"Who? Who has them?" Alistair asked.

"Lord Riverton, for his private library," Timothy said.

Winifred turned to Alistair. "Do you know him?"

Alistair nodded.

"Thank you for your time, Timothy." Winifred came to her feet.

"If we find you're lying to us, we'll be back, and next time I shall not be so kind," Alistair said. Then he smacked the boy on the back of his head. "Stop stealing from people. If you need funds, find employment."

She doubted that Alistair's threat would make much difference to Timothy. He was one of those who would always look for the easy way to do things, regardless of the legality or outcome.

Alistair gave an address to their driver and then assisted Winifred into the rig. Once they were back in the carriage, she asked, "Where are we going now?"

"Lord Riverton's."

"Now? We cannot simply show up whenever the mood strikes us. One must be invited." Alistair might be a marquess, but his social etiquette was lacking.

"Nonsense. He owns a private library and has a standing invitation to people to visit it. He loves showing off his treasures. And as I've said before—"

"Yes, this is work for his majesty," she provided. "It sounds as if you know Lord Riverton quite well."

Alistair's shoulders shifted in what she assumed was a shrug. "We went to school together."

They were quiet for several moments and she realized she'd be going out to a member of the ton's residence. Quite different from a boardinghouse in Southwark. She hadn't exactly been welcomed into society since Theodore had left her at the church. "Perhaps I should wait in the carriage," she said.

"No, I need you to come in with me, so he is not suspicious. The widow of the man who made his maps, he'll believe you want to see them," Alistair said.

"I suppose that does seem logical."

"You shall still masquerade as my betrothed." With that he pulled her to him and lowered his mouth to hers. His kiss was potent and passionate. Her lips parted and she welcomed him. Her arms slid around his neck and she leaned into him. Her body knew precisely what to do with Alistair—it was her mind that kept getting in the way.

Chapter Six

Alistair hadn't seen Jasper Riverton in more than fifteen years, but he needed those maps. He'd break into the man's house if he refused them entrance. The code needed to be deciphered and he was getting close. As much as he hated to admit it, having Winifred by his side gave him a jolt of courage—having her with him made him feel more comfortable about facing Riverton. Alistair didn't relish seeing anyone he'd gone to school with. At least those few in the Seven he'd known when he'd been a boy knew him now, knew his mind and respected his intelligence. But men like Riverton had only ever seen Alistair as a peculiarity.

Alistair had always been odd, even in his interactions with other peers of the realm. He spoke differently, when he bothered to talk; he moved differently; he certainly thought differently, which was why he was so damned good at his job. Of course it hadn't seemed that way growing up. Then he'd been ridiculed and teased as being a simpleton. It wasn't until Harrison, the leader of the Seven, recruited Alistair to break codes that Alistair had finally accepted his differences. Now he didn't give a damn what others thought of him. Except for Winifred.

The carriage rolled up toward the townhome. There were several other carriages in front, as well as people milling about.

"It appears as if his lordship is hosting a party," Winifred said.

"Indeed." That could be either good, a way for them to blend into the crowd, or bad, a damned school reunion.

"We will scarcely be noticed, I suspect," she said.

He could only hope. Oh how he loathed the small talk of London, conversing about the weather and the latest scandal or whatever political nonsense was going on in Parliament. He didn't give a fig about most of it. They were introduced into the house and no one seemed to blink at the sight of them. Riverton stood to the side with his wife. At least Alistair assumed the woman next to him was the man's wife.

Alistair stepped over to them, his hand resting on the small of Winifred's back. "Riverton," he said with a nod.

"Coventry, old boy." He grabbed Alistair in an embrace and popped him on the back.

Yet another reason to not enjoy London. People touched him too much. It was unsettling.

"I had no idea you ever came to London, else I would have sent an invitation. Glad you came by nonetheless." The man's eyes moved to Winifred, and his brows rose.

"Winifred Mirren," she said, introducing herself. "I am a friend of Lord Coventry's."

"Indeed," the man said with a waggle of his eyebrows. "Mirren, I know that name. You are the mapmaker's widow!" He clapped his hands together. "How splendid to make your acquaintance. I do hope you'll take the opportunity to peruse my collection of maps. I suspect you'll find it particularly interesting."

"Yes, I'd love to. Where might we find that?" she asked.

"Second floor, end of the west corridor," the man said,

pointing his finger toward the staircase.

Alistair nodded at the man again and ushered Winifred off.

"See how painless that was? You needn't be so afraid of people."

"I'm not *afraid* of them, I simply don't care for them." He glanced over at her. Her hand trailed against the railing as they climbed the stairs. "Most people."

She smiled, but did not look at him.

They made their way quietly to the collection room. That was the thing about Winifred; she was not disturbed by his silence. It used to drive Sarah to near madness. Or it finally had.

The moment they'd married, she'd begun peppering him with questions. It hadn't taken him long to realize that she could not be in a room with him for more than fifteen minutes before she'd start pestering him about his thoughts or his opinions about the gardens and whatnot.

Winifred, though, took his silence in stride, speaking when she wanted to, but not demanding he participate. It was the thing he liked most about her. And she was one of the very few people he'd encountered in life whom he felt able to simply be himself around. Not that he ever tried to be different with people, but with Winifred he wasn't as aware of his peculiarities.

She had an easy way about her with most people. Speaking to those who enjoyed conversation and as easily spending quiet moments with him. He found himself wondering what manner of relationship she and Mirren had had.

The collections room was large, big enough to host a soiree, but instead hosted shelves of books, large, framed maps, and several tables with other maps laid out.

"Good heavens, he is quite the collector," Winifred said. "I knew people liked Reggie's work, but I had no idea. I myself have always had a penchant for maps, but I thought that was merely a peculiar part of me." She smiled again.

His heart clenched. Those smiles were water to his

parched throat and he could not get enough of them. He needed to bed her soon else he begin to believe he needed her for something more than mere physical pleasure.

"Shall we begin?" she asked.

He inclined his head and started toward the maps hanging on the walls. "I need the Hook 1798, the Frost 1787, and the Baker 1792."

"Perfect." She moved effortlessly through the room, glancing at the ones on the walls first and then moving to the tables. "That Hook was always one of my favorites."

Alistair stepped over to a different table and looked through the maps sprawled on the top. Immediately he located the 1792. "Found one."

He withdrew the two books in his coat and found the appropriate coordinates for this map. Winifred brought him one of the other maps. As she placed it in front of him on the table, something caught his attention. He pulled this new map closer, then took a closer look at the first one.

"Have you found the third one?" he asked.

"I'm looking. What is it?"

"I'm not certain yet, but I believe these maps may have something hidden within them."

"What do you mean?"

"A secret coding or message."

"Well, that can't be. Reggie never did anything of the sort." She moved quickly through the other maps, found the third one he needed, and brought it over.

There it was, the same markings that the other two maps had. Hidden within the legend of the map there was yet another code. "See here, this symbol."

She leaned closer. "What is that? Some sort of insect?"

"That is a bee. A symbol of Napoleon's."

"What does that mean?"

"That someone was leaving messages here for traitors to

the Crown."

"Not Reggie," she said emphatically.

"No, I don't believe so. These were clearly added at a later date. The ink used is different."

"Timothy," she said.

"Perhaps. If he is involved, now that he knows we wanted these maps, he'll know we're on to him. We need to get out of here rather quickly."

"Get what you need first," she said. "I can look around to see if I find anything else of interest. Do I merely look for that little bee?"

Alistair gripped her arm. "I'm not certain we have time. Besides, I'm taking these maps with me. We'll need them for the investigation to see if Riverton is involved." Though Alistair doubted it. Riverton wasn't intelligent enough to be secretly working for Napoleon.

"Yes, they came up here a while ago, the marquess and his lady. They asked to look at my map collection," Riverton said from the corridor outside the room.

"We need to go. Now," Alistair said. He pulled her to a door at the back of the room, one that no doubt led to some sort of parlor. He was right, though the parlor seemed to be serving more as a storage room. It was lined with several pieces of furniture. He wove them through the maze of bureaus and tables and armoires until they reached the door. One peek into the corridor showed him the door to the collection room open.

He pulled Winifred out the door and off in the opposite direction.

Alistair needed to get word to Harrison, the leader of the Seven, that it was time to pick up Timothy to see what the apprentice really knew. More than likely, he was merely a pawn used by the real enemies in this game, but they couldn't be too certain. But first he needed to ensure Winifred was brought to safety.

Chapter Seven

By the time they reached the carriage, Winifred was winded. Someone had been looking for them. They hadn't stayed around to see who it was. Instead they'd sneaked out of the back of the Riverton home. She'd had to climb over plants and Alistair had pulled her over a stone wall that bordered their garden. But now he had her safely inside the carriage.

"I want to bring you to a friend's house where I know you can be protected," Alistair said once they started moving.

"No. I will not go anywhere without Oliver."

"Your son?"

"Yes. If I am in danger, then he might be in danger."

"Very well, we will pick him up. But you must be quick about it. I want you safely at Remy's so I can bring something to Harrison."

"Who is this Remy?"

"An associate. He also works for the Crown."

"If you trust him, then I shall as well." She reached into her reticule and pulled out a book. "This might be of use for your investigation."

"What is that?"

"The registry. A book that all the visitors to his library signed."

"We didn't sign in."

"We actually did. Well, I did, for us." She gave him a sheepish grin. "In any case, I thought that perhaps the list of signatures might assist in the investigation."

"Thank you, that was quite clever of you." She was clever. He'd always known it, he supposed, else she would have irritated him the way most people did. But he'd never really acknowledged it. She was intelligent and clever and damned if he hadn't put her in danger.

"Oh for pity's sake, doesn't this rig move any faster?" she said abruptly.

She was worried, he realized, for her boy. Her maternal side was unfamiliar, yet he found he didn't find it off-putting. Instead it was merely another facet of her to admire. "We are nearly there," he told her.

Fifteen minutes later, the carriage rolled to a stop and Winifred nearly jumped to the ground. They had almost made it to the front door when a sound caught Alistair's attention. He looked to the side. Behind some shrubberies to the left of her townhome lay a body.

Alistair swore.

Winifred ran to the form on the ground. "Gracious, it's Timothy!" Her hands flew over the man's chest, and red stained her fingers. "He's bleeding." She ripped a piece of fabric off the bottom of her skirt and did her best to press it against the wound.

"Shot. I've been shot," Timothy said, his voice hoarse. He coughed and sputtered.

There was no saving him with this much blood loss. "Who did this to you?" Alistair said.

He shook his head. "I don't—" Then a round of coughs.

He grabbed Winifred's arm. "Danger, you're in danger."

Cold fingers of dread scraped down Alistair's back. There was nothing to be done for Timothy, but Alistair could get Winifred to safety.

"Plimpson," Timothy said with another round of coughs. "I told him I sent you to Riverton."

"Winifred," Alistair said, bringing her to her feet. "There is nothing more to be done for him. You and your son need to be moved to safety. Now."

She took one last look at Timothy and nodded.

Ten minutes later, Alistair left Winifred's townhome with assurances from two of her footmen that they would see her safely to Remington's house. Alistair found Remy to be too boisterous for his liking, but he knew the man could be trusted. He had to alert Harrison to what had occurred so they could bring in this Plimpson for questioning. He'd quickly written a note to be given to Remy. Alistair needed to know when Winifred was safe.

Twenty minutes later, Alistair received notice of Winifred's safety while standing in Harrison's study. He had spent the last ten minutes filling in the leader of the Seven on the discoveries with the maps and the secret symbol. Harrison had left him to send messages to other members. Alistair had spent the time pacing, waiting.

Alistair read Remy's note again and allowed the relief to wash over him. He'd been so damned scared for her well-being. And damnation, that meant only one thing. He cared for her. Him, the man with virtually no emotional ties. But the thought of her being hurt made him crazy with anger and terrified him to his very core.

He'd thought her to be a nice diversion, an outlet for his physical needs, and instead she'd become the one person he cared about.

Chapter Eight

After Remy and his wife, Emma, had given Winifred and Oliver a nice welcome, insisting they stay the night, Winifred had put Oliver to bed. She sat in a chair outside of the bedchamber where Oliver slept. Timothy had been murdered, seemingly because she and Alistair had questioned him about maps. It all seemed so unreal.

Obviously he had alerted someone to the fact that they wanted to see those maps—Plimpson or whoever had commissioned Timothy to embed those secret codes. Codes for followers of Napoleon. Oh dear, sweet Reggie's maps. For the first time, she was thankful the man was dead, else the knowledge that someone was using his maps for ill would have certainly killed him.

He appeared in the corridor as if he'd known she needed to see him. She stood and nearly fell into his arms when he reached her. He kissed her head and kneaded the tense muscles in her back. Then he grabbed her hand and led her to another bedchamber a few doors down.

Once inside, he embraced her for several minutes, neither

of them speaking. His heart thundered beneath her ear, so strong, so steady. She tipped her head back and closed her eyes. Tonight was for her. A farewell to the only man she'd ever loved. She would always love him, she knew that now. Accepted it. He was the father of her child—how could she not love him? His seed had grown in her belly and become a beautiful, sweet, and smart boy she could not imagine her life without.

She should have known the fight would be futile. She'd waited six long years to be in Alistair's arms again. As his mouth moved against the column of her throat, all she could think was she had found where she belonged.

"I've missed you, Winifred. Your feel, your taste."

She said nothing, merely listened and felt. His hands held her tightly against him, resting on the small of her back. Protective, possessive. If only she were his. But she knew that could not be. She could have tonight, but that was all she could allow herself. If Alistair ever discovered the truth about Oliver, he'd never forgive her. He'd taken measures six years ago, as he would tonight, to prevent a pregnancy, but her body had betrayed them both. And though she didn't regret it, she knew he'd hate her for it.

She moved her hand up his chest and wanted to rip his clothes from him, wanted to feel his bare skin. She worked on the buttons and once she had an opening wide enough, she spread the fabric and flattened her palms on his chest. Warm, taut, and muscular, he was every bit as miraculous as she remembered him to be.

"I've missed you," she allowed herself to say. She dared not say too much, else she admit her feelings, give him her heart, and risk losing him for tonight.

Impatiently, he tore off his own shirt, perhaps as hungry for her touch as she was for his. The sight of his shoulders made her mouth dry. He was so beautiful.

He kissed her, his tongue coaxing, seducing. She was lost

to him. She kissed him back. Her hands moved to his back, and the play of the muscles there pulsed against her hands. Desire moved through her, igniting every limb, every inch of flesh.

Slowly he removed every piece of her clothing. He kissed each shoulder as he slid her chemise down. He moved to stand behind her and swept her hair aside. He kissed and nibbled at her throat, her neck. She closed her eyes and leaned into him. He reached around and cupped her breasts and her nipples, already hard, ached against his hands. She arched into him.

Warm flesh pressed against her back and she longed for the rest of him to be disrobed. She reached behind her and cupped his erection, and he leaned into her hand. But still he kissed her skin, loving her with his lips, his tongue, his hands.

Her skin flamed beneath his worship and impatience clawed at her. But he was in control, and she loved his lead.

His hands massaged her breasts, his erection pressed into her bottom, and she moved in a slow circle grinding against him, hoping she drove him as wild as he did her.

"Take off your breeches," she whispered.

"In time. I want to kiss every inch of you first." He led her to the bed. Then he kissed her back, down the center of her spine, her hips, her waist, the tender spot where her bottom met her legs. She would not be able to withstand much longer. "Alistair, please," she begged.

"Patience, love." A kiss behind each knee, her thighs, her calves, then his hands ran up both legs and stopped on her bottom. "You have a sweet bottom, do you know that?"

She smiled, but said nothing. His torture didn't end there. He started at her feet and kissed his way up to her knees, nibbled at her inner thighs. Then licked his way up to the apex of her thighs. She sucked in her breath and instinctively clenched her legs together.

"Relax," he whispered. His breath feathered through the triangle of hair. His hands ran up the length of her thighs and settled in the middle where all her desire pooled. "Has anyone ever kissed you here?"

Her eyes widened. "No, never." No one had ever been down there but him. But she didn't tell him that.

He lowered his mouth and put his lips on her. Then he parted her curls and kissed her most sensitive part. She sucked in her breath and nearly floated off the bed.

"Oh my," she said. It was her last coherent thought as her body flooded with sensations. He kissed and suckled and licked, and she writhed and moaned and shivered. Pleasure exploded through her when he slipped a finger inside. "Now, oh please, now."

He chuckled, a low and deep seductive laugh that sent shivers through her. He stood from the bed. The remainder of his clothes hit the floor, and then he was on top of her, the pressure of his body against hers...oh how she'd missed him. She knew he'd taken precautions again, his attempt to prevent another pregnancy. She wanted to tell him that his efforts were in vain, that his efforts weren't foolproof, weren't a guarantee, but then in one swift movement, he entered her. And her pleasure mounted again with every thrust.

She lifted her legs and wrapped them around his back, deepening his penetration. Her climax hit hard and fast, right before his abdomen tightened and he groaned with his release.

Never had she felt so close to someone, so connected. They were one flesh. In that moment she allowed herself to fantasize what could happen if she told him about Oliver. He'd smile broadly and pull her against him, profess his love as she professed hers, and they'd be a family, finally together.

Now, though, he merely rolled off of her and pulled her close to him. "I told you we're good together."

She traced her finger down the scar that crossed his left cheek and ran down his throat onto his chest. She'd always wondered what had caused it, but she'd never dared ask. Not because she didn't think he'd tell her, but because she knew he would and whatever had caused this angry mark would remind her all too much of the danger he had faced when he'd fought in the war.

"Is this from the war?"

"No," he said, but offered no further explanation.

She hadn't realized that giving herself to Alistair again would make her feel so strongly about telling him about Oliver. But she felt so open, so exposed, she had to fight the words from tumbling out. She snuggled closer to him, searching for a way to bring up the topic. "Why were you so surprised when you discovered I had a child?"

His shoulders shrugged under her. "I suppose since I've never wanted children, I forget that other people might."

"Do you not like children?"

"I've never really been around them. I mean I was when I was a child, but not since," he said, his tone tighter.

She chewed at her lip. "Then why the adamant feelings against them?"

He sat abruptly, his jaw clenched. "You want to know what this scar is?" He dragged his finger against the puckered skin. "I tried to save her, my wife, when she jumped from the cliff. I fell onto ragged rocks and missed her," he said hoarsely.

People assumed he had killed his wife, but evidently she'd killed herself and he'd been there, seen it, tried to stop her.

"She is the reason for the scar and why I carry a cane. I don't limp anymore, but I did for so long." He exhaled slowly. "And she is the reason I do not want children."

The hope Winifred had felt just moments before dissolved into a tight knot in her belly. Even more she knew she could not ever tell him, could not ever let him know that his child already existed.

Chapter Nine

Alistair slipped from the bed and donned his clothes. Winifred slept deeply, her breathing even and calm. Momentarily he thought to kiss her head before he crept from her room, but instead he merely turned and left. The stairs to the first floor were just around the corner, but something caught his eye.

A boy stood down the corridor, small, wide-eyed, one hand on the doorknob to what Alistair assumed was the boy's sleeping chamber.

Alistair took a step toward him. "Are you looking for your mother?"

The boy shook his head.

"Do you need anything?"

He merely looked up at Alistair with his big, green eyes. Eyes that seemed oddly familiar. With one more glance, the boy opened his door and slipped inside.

Alistair turned to go. Winifred's son. He'd seen glimpses these past few days of what she was like as a mother. She was obviously concerned with the boy's education and his safety. No doubt she was comforting and loving. Everything his own mother had not been. She'd thought him peculiar and simple. Oliver was a fortunate boy to have such a loving mother.

• • •

When she'd woken up that morning and found Alistair gone, and the bed where he'd been cold and empty, Winifred realized she could not continue their relationship. Being in his arms was wonderful, but the aftermath when he was vacant was too much for her to endure again and again. She wanted all or nothing and she shouldn't have to settle for anything less.

Remy and Emma's hospitality had been welcoming, and for a moment she'd entertained the thought of the four of them dining together, laughing at the adventures in spying. But that entire scenario was ludicrous. Winifred had to face that there would never be a future between her and Alistair. So as soon as Remy told her that her house had been secured and guards placed around it, she took Oliver home.

She'd been told that Alistair had already arrived and was at work in the map room, earnestly trying to decipher the code. She knew that she needed to talk to him, to cut things off with him and end their would-be affair.

She bolstered her courage to tell him precisely that.

He was diligently writing when she entered the room, but he lifted his head and gave her a slight smile. "I trust you slept well."

She had, better than she'd slept in years, until she'd realized him gone.

"I cannot have an affair with you," she said quickly before she lost her nerve.

"I believe you already have. Twice."

"Yes, well, that is all. I will not keep doing this." She hadn't walked any farther into the room so the distance between them was vast, her by the door and him all the way at the far table.

"What are you trying to tell me?"

"You have no notion how very difficult it was for me that first time. To try and forget you." She tried her best not to wring her hands, but her efforts were futile.

"You married rather quickly, so I doubt that my memory plagued you for too long."

It was on her tongue to tell him that she'd grown rather fond of him. Perhaps she'd even fallen in love with him. Loved him still. "I know that you do not feel the same and I am not asking you to. But you storm into my life and leave a wake of pain when you leave. It's wonderful while you're here, but the after?" Her shoulders wilted. "I simply cannot put those pieces back together."

"You were younger then, much less worldly. I suspect you fancied yourself in love when truly it was merely the blush of losing your virginity."

He was so coarse sometimes. Hurtful when she knew he didn't intend to be. It was simply his way.

"What if I do not wish to let you go?" he asked.

She dared take several steps farther into the room. "You can offer me nights of wonder, pleasures that I can scarcely imagine. But in the mornings, I'm left with an empty and cold bed. It is more than I can endure."

"So you would rather be alone all the time than merely alone in the mornings?"

She gave him a wistful smile. "Precisely."

"That makes no sense, Winifred."

"Perhaps. But I must do what I must."

He was quiet for a few moments, then said, "I spoke to your son last night."

Her heart stopped. "You did?"

"On my way out of your room, he was standing in the

corridor. He didn't say anything."

"He doesn't."

"He is bashful, then?"

"No, he doesn't talk. Yet." She nodded, but was unsure if she was trying to convince Alistair or herself. "But I know it is only a matter of time."

He looked up at her, his face pale. "I have to go." He gathered his materials.

"Are you finished with the code?"

"Nearly." And with that he left the room. Left her alone. Again.

• • •

Alistair had left shortly after the exchange with Winifred. He was quite close to deciphering the remainder of the code in the book, and in the process had made a truly disturbing discovery. But he'd had to get away from Winifred. He needed to be alone. To think.

But that wasn't going to happen. When he got to his townhome, he was informed that Remy was there. Alistair stepped into his study. He might not be interested in a social call, but Remy's presence would solve one problem. He could tell him what he'd discovered about the journal. Alistair didn't know about everyone in the Seven, but he knew he trusted Remy.

"I've already talked to Harrison about my discoveries, but you might as well know, too," Alistair said.

Remy waved his hand. "No, I came to talk about something else."

"I'm not in the mood for a social call."

"It matters not what you're in the mood for. There are things we need to discuss."

"I decode the journal, that's the extent of my involvement

in these investigations, you know that." He took a seat behind the desk. "But I do trust you, which is why I will tell you a disturbing thing I have discovered while working with Comfry's journal. I'm fairly certain that the main traitor we seek, the one we've been commissioned to find, is a member of the Seven."

Remy frowned. "You're quite serious."

"I'm always serious."

"Be that as it may, that is not why I am here, though obviously this news needs to get to Harrison straightaway."

"Why are you here, then?" Alistair asked.

Remy eyed him for a minute or so, then rubbed the back of his neck. "Tell me you haven't completely missed it? You, who notice nearly everything the rest of us never notice."

"What the devil are you talking about?"

"The boy, Alistair, certainly you've noticed the similarities. For Christ's sake, he looks like you. Not to mention the mannerisms." He blew out a breath. "I would have known he was your son anywhere."

The room tilted and Alistair focused on Remy's words. Of course he'd begun to suspect that very thing, but to hear the words "your son" was too much...

"Why didn't you ever tell us you had a child?"

"I—I didn't know."

Remy released a curse. "She hasn't told you."

All Alistair could do was shake his head. But then a thought hit him and he came to his feet. "I need to go."

"Of course. Obviously you and Winifred have much to discuss. I'm sorry, I didn't realize—"

But Alistair slipped out of the room before he could hear more. At the moment he had nothing to say to Winifred.

It took nearly twenty minutes for the carriage to get him to the Piccadilly area. Alistair slammed the knocker onto the door of one Mr. Bellford. The man appeared shortly thereafter.

"My lord," he said, obviously surprised at Alistair's visit. "How may I help you?"

"I have questions," he demanded.

The man granted him entrance and led him to a small study. "Do you wish for tea?"

"No. What are you tutoring the boy? What are you teaching him?"

The man's eyebrows rounded. "I thought you knew. Your letter was quite insistent that I take this position. I assumed you knew... He does not speak. I've had some luck with such cases."

"He does not speak at all?"

"No, my lord."

Panic seized Alistair, but he forced out the next question. "Is he a simpleton?"

The man smiled warmly. "Quite the opposite. He is remarkably intelligent. Can already do arithmetic and knows how to read. He simply does not speak the words, though I suspect he knows plenty of them."

Alistair fell into the chair behind him and stared at the fireplace void of any flames. Now he knew why those eyes looked so damned familiar. Winifred's son. His son.

"I believe the boy will speak eventually, he merely hasn't needed to at this point."

It wasn't that simple, Alistair knew that, but he nodded. "Thank you for your time." Then he stood and left. Now he was ready to speak to Winifred. It was time she told him the truth.

• • •

Winifred pulled Oliver closer to her. "Were you out looking for me last night, my sweet?" she asked.

He shook his head.

"I know you met one of Maman's friends. Were you not sleeping?"

He tapped on the book.

She fought off the frustration at his silence. She knew he could talk if he wanted to, and sometimes she got so angry. But patience was the key. She opened the book and began reading. He snuggled in closer to her.

A commotion came from the corridor and then the door opened.

"My lady, I tried to stop him, but he was rather insistent," Polly said.

Alistair stood there looking far more harried than she'd ever seen him. His eyes fell to the boy nestled to her and the muscles in his jaw ticked. "A moment, please, Winifred."

"Polly, take Oliver upstairs. We shall finish this book later, my sweet."

Oliver stood and stared at Alistair, then scurried out of the room.

Alistair's eyes turned to her. "How could you?"

He knew. The room spun around her and she was thankful she still sat. She concentrated on breathing. In and out. In and out.

"Damnation woman, answer me! The boy is mine, isn't he?"

She nodded. "I tried to tell you. Once."

His head cocked to one side and one eyebrow lifted. "I don't recall."

"You were not there. I went to your castle, but you were away, working on some assignment, they told me." She stood, but didn't dare step any closer to him. She'd never seen him angry, so full of emotion. "Being at Coventry Hall reminded me of our time together and all of the things you told me. You were quite specific when we made love that there was not to be a child. You took precautions."

"Precautions that are quite obviously not foolproof."

"Obviously." He was quiet for a moment and she put her hand on his forearm. "Alistair, you don't need to do anything. You never wanted children, you need not feel obligated—"

"You don't understand!" he said louder than he'd intended. "That thing that is wrong with your boy, I did that to him." He jammed a finger in his chest.

Realization crashed over her. "That's what you believe? That you're somehow defective? Is that what your wife told you?"

He looked up at her, raw emotion etched in his features. She would remember that face the rest of her life. It was nothing but pure anguish. "Who hurt you so badly?" she whispered.

"I do not need nor want your pity." He stormed out of the room.

Since the moment she'd discovered she carried his child, she'd imagined many scenarios in which they'd have this discussion. None of her imaginings could have prepared her for this.

Chapter Ten

Winifred paced the length of rug laid out in the corridor of Remy and Emma's home. It was the first time she'd even known Alistair had friends, and she was grateful she'd met them. The butler had gone to retrieve them since Winifred had explained that it was an emergency that she speak with them.

Remy was the first one down the stairs. "Is everything all right with Alistair?"

She shook her head. "He's not injured, if that's what you mean." She took a sobering breath. "Could I ask you some questions about him?"

He gave her a kind smile and led her to a parlor. "Sit, I'll ring for tea."

"That won't be necessary. I spoke with him and he knows that my son is his son and, well, he's obviously quite angry with me for keeping such a secret."

"I might have had something to do with that. I didn't realize he didn't know." He squeezed her hand. "I am truly sorry for that."

"It matters not now. And he deserved to know the truth, I was simply too scared to tell him myself." She frowned. "He said that the thing that is wrong with my boy came from him. I don't know what he's talking about."

"The not speaking," Remy said.

"Yes, but how could Alistair have done that to him?"

"Alistair is a peculiar fellow. Certainly you've noticed that."

She managed a small smile. "He is different, I suppose, but he's intelligent and passionate and can be humorous, when he wants to be."

"I don't know the full story, but I've heard that he was quite old before he spoke. His parents believed him a simpleton and sent him off to live with his grandfather. The old man was patient with him, kind and gentle, and eventually Alistair learned to speak, but he's always been the way he is."

"He was afraid of passing on his speech issues to children, I can understand that, but he seemed quite…"

"His wife, she killed herself."

"Yes, I know that much. Though many believe he pushed her."

"People say foolish things to create scandal where there is none. And Alistair feeds those rumors because he's reclusive and aloof."

That certainly made sense.

"She jumped off that cliff, though, because she got pregnant. She told him she couldn't bear the thought of birthing a creature like him."

Her heart shattered at the words. Poor, dear Alistair had been terrified of getting another woman pregnant. "That was very unkind of her."

"That's a mild understatement," Remy said. "She was a nasty woman. I never cared for her myself. She was the younger sister of one of my friends. Sarah was selfish and superficial. She hated Alistair because he didn't spend his life worshiping her, telling her how beautiful she was. I suspect she would have tossed herself off a cliff no matter whom she married. No man would have ever been enough for her. But Alistair will never see it that way."

"Of course not."

"Give him some time. I'm certain he'll come around. It is quite obvious that he loves you. He merely needs time to come to terms with that." He chuckled. "Alistair has believed for a long time that he's above the baser emotions of us mortals. And it certainly took a very special woman to crack into his heart."

"I doubt that, but it is certainly kind of you to say." She gave Remy a smile.

Remy squeezed her hand. "You love him, do you not?"

"Yes, I have for years." She had suspected all along that she'd loved him, but it seemed ridiculous to fancy herself in love with someone she'd had a brief affair with years ago. But she knew now, without a doubt, that Alistair Devlin had her heart. It was hard to not be in love with him when she saw him reflected in her son's face every day.

"Don't give up on him."

She wouldn't, but she felt certain that Alistair had already given up on her.

Two weeks passed and she heard nothing from Alistair. Then out of nowhere, he sent a carriage for her and Oliver requesting their presence at his townhome. Once they arrived, she was ushered into a parlor, but the butler led Oliver to meet Alistair somewhere else.

When her boy looked at her over his shoulder, uncertain of what to do, she gave him a warm smile.

"Go ahead, my sweet. I shall be right here waiting for you."
He nodded and left.

In the weeks that had passed, she had taken the time to tell Oliver the truth about his father. She hoped one day that Alistair would want to be a part of the boy's life, but she didn't make Oliver any promises. He had seemed confused at first, but as the days progressed, he'd warmed to the idea and had started asking when he could see Alistair again. Well, he'd asked in his way, sitting in the window and watching and waiting.

She waited ten minutes before going to find them. After searching the first floor, she eventually found them in a room on the second floor when she heard Alistair's voice. She did not enter, merely stood in the corridor outside the room.

"Do you understand what I'm telling you, Oliver?"

Oliver must have nodded because Alistair replied, "Good. I know it is difficult, but you mustn't get too discouraged. Do you see all of these tools and books that I have? I use them for a very important task for the King. Did you know that I work for His Majesty? It is very important work, and because my mind works differently than other people's, I am able to do things that they cannot do."

Tears pricked at Winifred's eyes. She'd been so afraid of Alistair's reaction that she'd never stopped to realize that the very person she'd hid Oliver from might be the one person who could help him most. She'd been selfish and a fool.

"Other people don't understand us, Oliver. We can't blame them for it, their minds are simply not as clever as ours."

She smiled through her tears. She wished she could be in the room, see both of their faces. The two people she loved most in the world, together.

"And then I found someone who does understand me, but I ruined things because I was angry and hurt."

There was a tight cough, and then, "What...what if?" Oliver asked. His little voice stumbled over the syllables, but it was the most beautiful voice she'd ever heard.

Tears streamed down Winifred's face and she fought the urge to run into the room. She clasped her hand over her mouth. Her boy had spoken. His words weren't perfect, but his sweet voice poured over her, a healing balm.

"What if you don't find someone who understands you?" Alistair asked.

There was a pause. Oliver must have nodded.

"That's it though, boy, you already have someone. And she loves you and understands you in a way that no one ever will. You are so fortunate because you get to spend every day with her."

Oliver coughed again, but he said nothing more.

"But I ruined things with her. I never told her how much she meant to me."

She stepped into the room. "You could tell me now."

"Winifred?" Alistair said, coming to his feet.

Oliver ran to her and she knelt and gathered her son into her arms. "I love you, my sweet."

"Love," he said with a nod.

Alistair came over to them, wrapped one arm around her waist, and put the other on Oliver's cheek. "Winifred, I have been an idiot."

"No, you didn't know. There was no way for you to know."

"That's not what I mean. I should never have let you go six years ago. I knew you were different, knew that you stirred something deep inside me, but I did nothing. I love you."

"Truly?" she asked.

He nodded

"Certainly you must know I love you."

"I do." He kissed her lips briefly. "How do you feel about being married to a man with a mysterious reputation?"

"I thought you'd never ask."

About the Author

National Bestselling author Robyn DeHart's novels have appeared in the top bestselling romance and historical romance lists. Her books have been translated into nearly a dozen languages. Her historical romantic adventure series, *The Legend Hunters*, were not only bestsellers, but also award winners, snagging a Reader's Crown and a Reviewer's Choice award. She'll have four releases in 2014 and already has three on the calendar for 2015, all set in the popular historical romance Regency and Victorian eras.

Known for her "strong dialogue and characters that leap off the page" (*RT Bookclub*) and her "sizzling romance" (*Publishers Weekly*), her books have been featured in *USA Today* and the *Chicago Tribune*. A popular writing instructor, she has given speeches at writing conferences in Los Angeles, Washington DC, New York, Dallas, Nashville, and Toronto, among many others.

When not writing, you can find Robyn hanging out with her family, husband (The Professor) a university professor of Political Science, and their two ridiculously beautiful and smart daughters, Busybee and Babybee, as well as two spoiled-rotten cats. They live in the hill country of Texas where it's hot eight months of the year, but those big blue skies make it worth it.

Don't miss the Masquerading Mistresses series...

NO ORDINARY MISTRESS
MISADVENTURES IN SEDUCTION
MASQUERADING MISTRESSES BUNDLE

Also by Robyn DeHart...

FORBIDDEN LOVE SERIES

A LITTLE BIT WICKED
A LITTLE BIT SINFUL
A LITTLE BIT SCANDALOUS
FORBIDDEN LOVE BUNDLE

BROTHERHOOD OF THE SWORD SERIES

UNDERCOVER WITH THE EARL
DUELING WITH THE DUKE
ELOPING WITH THE PRINCESS

LORDS OF VICE SERIES

THE SCOUNDREL AND THE LADY
THE MARQUESS AND THE MAIDEN
THE EARL AND THE RELUCTANT LADY
THE VIRGIN AND THE VISCOUNT

Discover more romance from Entangled...

A HIGHLAND ROGUE TO RUIN
a Highland Handfasts novel by E. Elizabeth Watson

Tormund MacLeod only wants vengeance for his brother's murder. But the Lughnasadh festival offers many distractions—including a fair and bonny masked vixen whose touch disarms him. Lady Brighde MacDonald might understand her brother's overprotectiveness—but what she needs is the reckless freedom in the arms of a Highlander. Only too late, they both recognize that they're enemies. Now their tryst could mean war. And Tormund hides a long-buried secret that could destroy both clans.

THE DUKE'S SECRET CINDERELLA
a Never a Wallflower novel by Eva Devon

Charlotte Browne could just kick herself. What possessed her to tell the Duke of Rockford that she is a lady? She's just plain Charlotte—with cinder-stained hands, a wretched stepfather, and no prospects. After one illicit kiss from the duke, Charlotte flees, leaving only a blue ribbon behind. The duke's touch may heat her skin, her very soul, but he can never know who she truly is...especially when even she doesn't know the truth.

THE HIGHLANDER'S ENCHANTRESS
a novel by Violetta Rand

If her cruel and domineering father were to be believed, Kali Bane is the worst of women. Defiant. Independent. When she refuses to wed, her father bans her to the McKay clan in the Highlands, warning them that she's a witch. Here she is little more than a hostage, kept from sight from almost all but Adam McKay, the laird's son. The longer she remains imprisoned in the McKay tower, the more Kali and Adam realize there are other forces at play. They're both pieces in a silent, terrible game that could destroy everyone they've ever loved...including each other.